ARTFOLDS

....

THIS BOOK BELONGS TO

....

FOLDED BY

CLASSIC EDITIONS

STAR WARS

DARTH VADER: THE DARK LORD

STUDIO FUN

WHITE PLAINS, NEW YORK • MONTRÉAL, QUÉBEC • BATH, UNITED KINGDOM

ArtFolds®
Classic Editions
Darth Vader: The Dark Lord
© AND ™ 2015 LUCASFILM LTD.

ArtFolds is a patent-pending process.

Copyright ©2015 by Studio Fun International, Inc.
Copyright ©2015 by Studio Fun International Limited

Studio Fun Books is a trademark and ArtFolds is a
registered trademark of Studio Fun International, Inc.,
a subsidiary of The Reader's Digest Association, Inc.

ISBN 978-0-7944-3491-5

To learn more about ArtFolds, visit www.artfolds.com.

Customized and/or prefolded ArtFolds are available. To explore options and
pricing, email specialorder@artfolds.com.

To discover the wide range of products available from Studio Fun
International, visit www.studiofun.com.

Address any comments about ArtFolds to:
Publisher
Studio Fun Books
44 South Broadway, 7th floor
White Plains, NY 10601
Or send an email to publisher@artfolds.com.

Printed in China   Conforms to ASTM F963

1 3 5 7 9 10 8 6 4 2   LPP/05/15

About ArtFolds

THE BOOK YOU HOLD IN YOUR HANDS is more than just a book. It's an ArtFolds! Inside are simple instructions that will show you how to fold pages to transform this book into a beautiful sculpture. No special skill is required; all you'll do is carefully fold the corners of marked book pages, based on the markings provided. When complete, you'll have created a long-lasting work of art. It's fun and easy, and can be completed in just one evening!

To add to the experience, each ArtFolds contains compelling reading content. In this edition, you'll experience the dark side of the Force, in the words of its adherents and its enemies.

Each ArtFolds edition is designed by an established, professional book sculptor whose works are displayed and sold in art galleries, museum shops, and online crafts and art stores. ArtFolds celebrates this community of artists, and encourages you to support this expanding art form by seeking out their work and sharing their unique designs and creations with others.

To learn more about ArtFolds, visit artfolds.com. There you'll find details of all ArtFolds editions, instructional videos, and much more.

Instructions

Creating your ArtFolds® Classic Edition book sculpture is easy! Just follow these simple instructions and guidelines:

1. Always fold right-hand pages.

2. Always fold toward you.

3. All folding pages require two folds: The top corner will fold down, and the bottom corner will fold up.

4. Grasp the top right corner of the page, and fold until the side of the page aligns exactly with the TOP black line.

5. Grasp the bottom right corner of the page, and fold upward until the side of the page aligns exactly with the BOTTOM black line.

6. Run your finger across the folds to make sure they are straight, crisp and accurate.

7. If the folded corner goes past the center crease of the book, simply fold back the paper that extends past the crease so the page can turn normally.

8. Continue on to the next page and repeat until your ArtFolds book sculpture is complete!

Extra Advice

- We recommend washing and then thoroughly drying your hands prior to folding.

- Some folders prefer using a tool to help make fold lines straight and sharp. Bone folders, metal rulers, popsicle sticks, or any other firm, straight tool will work.

- Some folders prefer to rotate their book sideways to make folding easier.

- Remember: The more accurate you are with each fold, the more accurate your completed book sculpture will be!

- Right after the book has been folded, it may fan out broadly. To compress the sculpture, close it and wrap it in a couple of rubber bands for a day or two.

Folding begins in just a few pages—look out for the folding guidelines on the right-hand page.

For more folding instructions and videos, visit artfolds.com.

Darth Vader: The Dark Lord

FOR OVER A THOUSAND YEARS, the Dark Lords of the Sith—followers of the dark side of the Force—manipulated galactic events in the shadows. Following the teachings of Darth Bane, there were only two Sith Lords in existence at a time—a Master and an apprentice. In secret, the Sith created unrest in the galaxy, plotting the downfall of their sworn enemies, the Jedi. Only when Darth Sidious took over the role of Master did their plan for domination come to the attention of the Jedi—and by then it was too late. The Sith had undermined the very foundations of the Galactic Republic, and their path to power was already underway. When Darth Sidious finally defeated the Jedi and took control of the Republic, he renamed it the Empire. He also took a new apprentice, whom he named Darth Vader. Together, they ruled the galaxy through fear. Here you can experience their story, through their own words and the words of their supporters and foes.

Darth Sidious: "Viceroy, I don't want this stunted slime in my sight again."

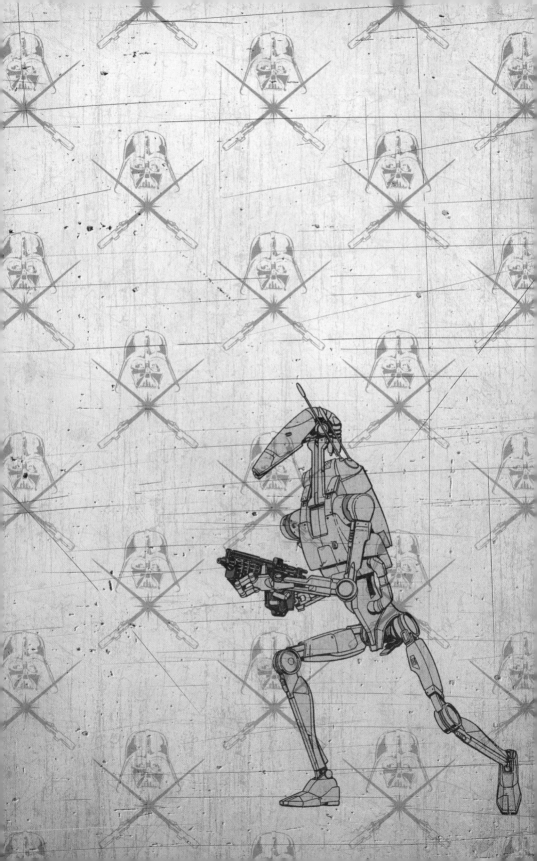

Darth Sidious: "Move
against the Jedi first."

Darth Sidious: "Queen Amidala is young and naïve. You will find controlling her will not be difficult."

Darth Sidious: "And Queen Amidala, has she signed the treaty?"

Nute Gunray: "She has disappeared, my Lord. One Naboo cruiser got past the blockade."

Darth Sidious: "I want that treaty signed."

Nute Gunray: "My Lord, it's impossible to locate the ship. It's out of our range."

Darth Sidious: "Not for a Sith…"

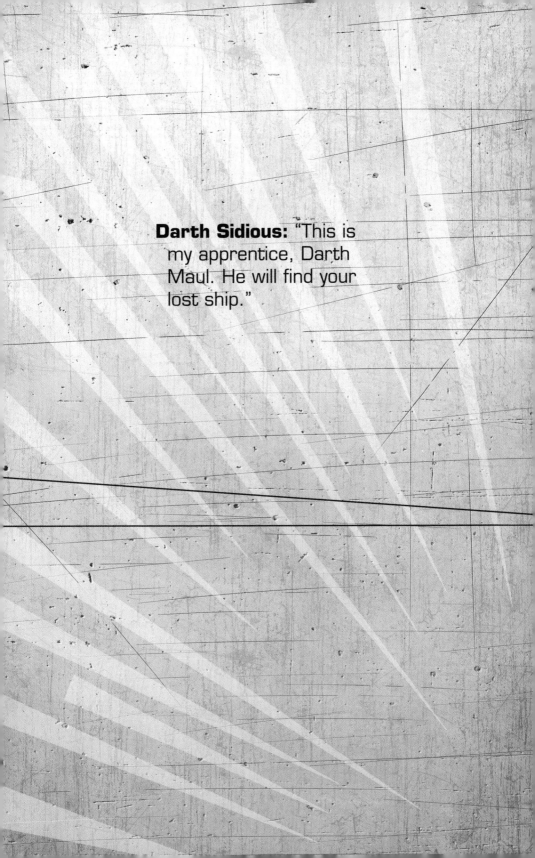

Darth Sidious: "This is my apprentice, Darth Maul. He will find your lost ship."

Darth Maul: "Tatooine is sparsely populated. If the trace was correct, I will find them quickly, Master."

Darth Sidious: "…you will then have no difficulty taking the queen back to Naboo to sign the treaty."

Darth Maul: "At last we will reveal ourselves to the Jedi. At last we will have revenge."

Darth Sidious: "You have been well trained, my young apprentice, they will be no match for you."

Qui-Gon Jinn: "My only conclusion can be that it was a Sith Lord."
Mace Windu: "A Sith Lord?!?"
Ki-Adi-Mundi: "Impossible! The Sith have been extinct for a millennium."

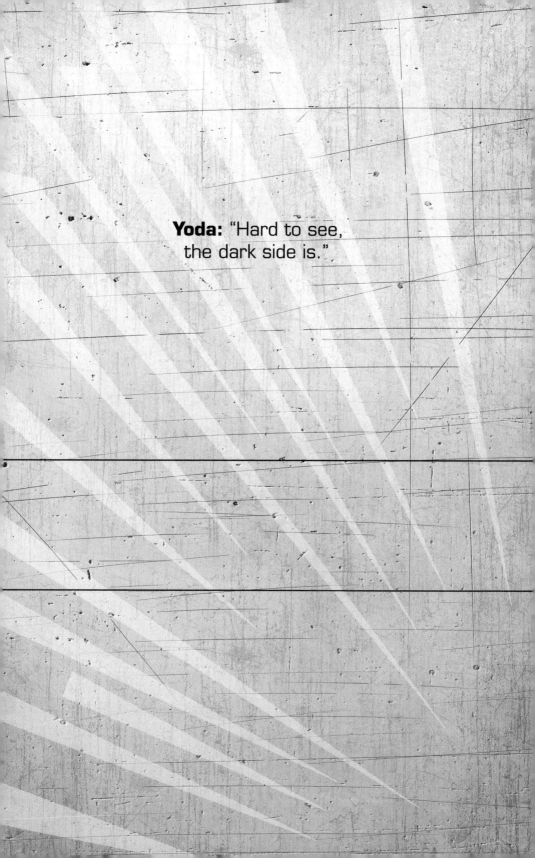

Yoda: "Hard to see,
the dark side is."

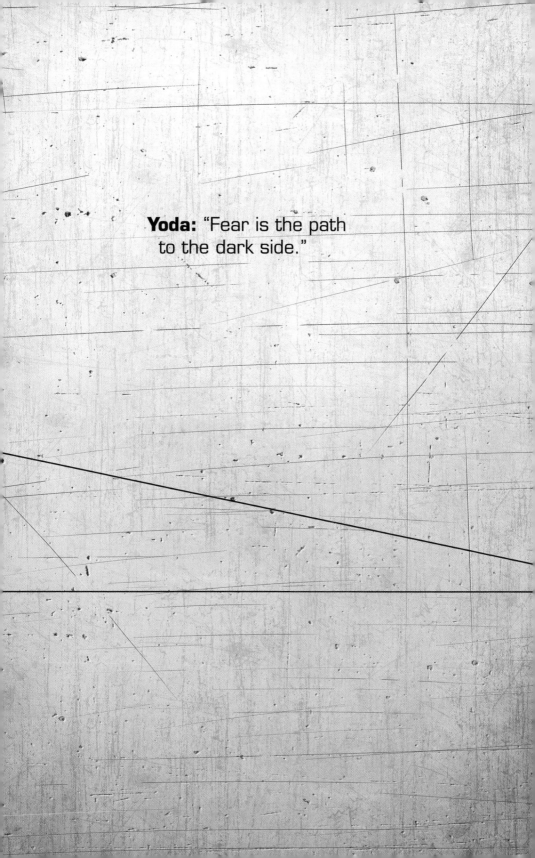

Yoda: "Fear is the path to the dark side."

Yoda: "Fear leads to anger."

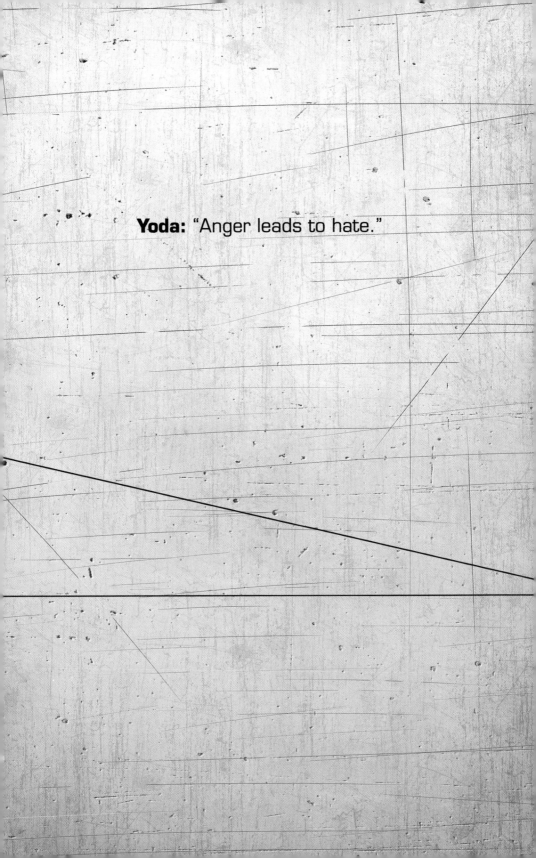

Yoda: "Anger leads to hate."

Yoda: "Hate leads to suffering."

Yoda: "I sense much fear in you."

Mace Windu: "Go with the queen to Naboo and discover the identity of the dark warrior. That is the clue we need to unravel this mystery of the Sith."

Darth Sidious: "Wipe them out…
all of them."

Mace Windu: "There is no doubt. The mysterious warrior was a Sith."

Yoda: "Always two there are…no more…no less. A master and an apprentice."

Mace Windu: "But which one was destroyed, the master or the apprentice?"

Yoda: "The dark side clouds everything."

Obi-Wan Kenobi: "Why do I think you are going to be the death of me?"

Count Dooku: "May I ask why a Jedi Knight is all the way out here on Geonosis?"

Count Dooku: "It's a great pity our paths have never crossed before, Obi-Wan. Qui-Gon Jinn always spoke very highly of you."

Count Dooku: "What if I told you that the Republic is now under control of a Dark Lord of the Sith?"
Obi-Wan Kenobi: "No, that's not possible. The Jedi would be aware of it."

Count Dooku: "The dark side of the Force has clouded their vision, my friend."

Count Dooku: "Hundreds of senators are now under the influence of a Sith Lord called Darth Sidious."

Obi-Wan Kenobi: "I don't believe you."

Count Dooku: "You must join me, Obi-Wan, and together we will destroy the Sith!"

Count Dooku: "Master Kenobi, you disappoint me. Yoda holds you in such high esteem."

Anakin Skywalker: "You're going to pay for all of the Jedi that you killed today, Dooku."

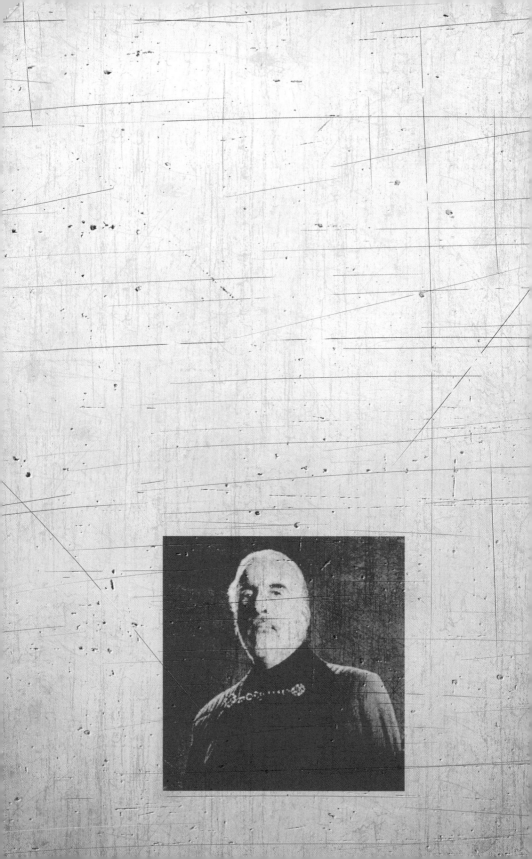

Count Dooku: "As you see, my
Jedi powers are far beyond
yours. Now back down."

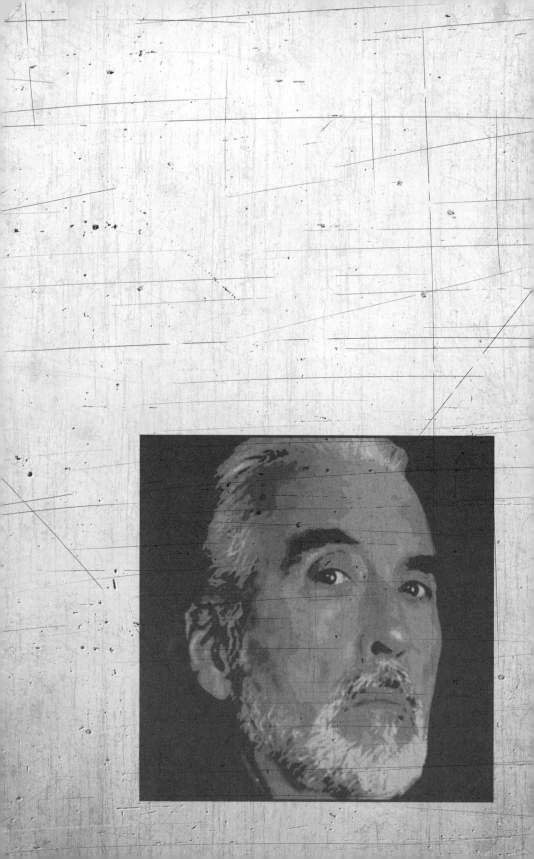

Count Dooku: "Surely
you can do better!"

Count Dooku: "Brave of you, boy—but
I would have thought you'd learned
your lesson."
Anakin Skywalker: "I am a slow learner..."

Count Dooku: "You have interfered with our affairs for the last time."

Yoda: "Powerful you have become, Dooku. The dark side I sense in you."

Count Dooku: "I've become more powerful than any Jedi. Even you."

Yoda: "Much to learn you still have."
Count Dooku: "It is obvious that this
contest cannot be decided by our
knowledge of the Force but by our
skills with a lightsaber."

Count Dooku: "The Force is with us, Master Sidious."

Darth Sidious: "Welcome home, Lord Tyranus. You have done well."

Darth Tyranus: "I have good news for you, my Lord. The war has begun."
Darth Sidious: "Excellent. Everything is going as planned."

Obi-Wan Kenobi: "Do you believe what Count Dooku said about Sidious controlling the Senate? It doesn't feel right."

Yoda: "Joined the dark side, Dooku has. Lies, deceit, creating mistrust are his ways now."

Chancellor Palpatine: "Get help! You're no match for him. He's a Sith Lord."

Obi-Wan Kenobi: "Chancellor Palpatine, Sith Lords are our specialty."

Count Dooku: "Your swords, please.
We don't want to make a mess of
things in front of the Chancellor."
Obi-Wan Kenobi: "You won't get
away this time, Dooku."

Count Dooku: "I've been looking forward to this."

Anakin Skywalker: "My powers have doubled since the last time we met, Count."

Count Dooku: "Good! Twice the pride, double the fall."

Count Dooku: "I sense great fear in you, Skywalker."

Count Dooku: "You have hate, you have anger…but you don't use them."

Darth Sidious: "General Grievous, I suggest you move the Separatist leaders to Mustafar."

General Grievous: "It will be done, my Lord."

Darth Sidious: "The end of the war is near, General."

General Grievous: "But…the loss of Count Dooku!"

Darth Sidious: "His death was a necessary loss. Soon I will have a new apprentice—one far younger and more powerful."

Chancellor Palpatine: "All who gain power are afraid to lose it. Even the Jedi."

Anakin Skywalker: "The Jedi use their power for good."

Chancellor Palpatine: "Good is a point of view, Anakin."

Chancellor Palpatine: "The Sith and the Jedi are almost the same in every way, including their quest for greater power."

Anakin Skywalker: "The Sith rely on their passions for their strength. They think inwards, only about themselves."

Chancellor Palpatine: "Did you ever hear the tragedy of Darth Plagueis the Wise?"

Anakin Skywalker: "No."

Chancellor Palpatine: "I thought not. It's not a story the Jedi would tell you. It's a Sith legend. Darth Plagueis was a Dark Lord of the Sith so powerful and so wise he could use the Force to influence the midi-chlorians to create life. He had such a knowledge of the dark side he could even keep the ones he cared about from dying."

Anakin Skywalker: "He could actually save people from death?"

Chancellor Palpatine: "The dark side of the Force is a pathway to many abilities some would consider to be unnatural."

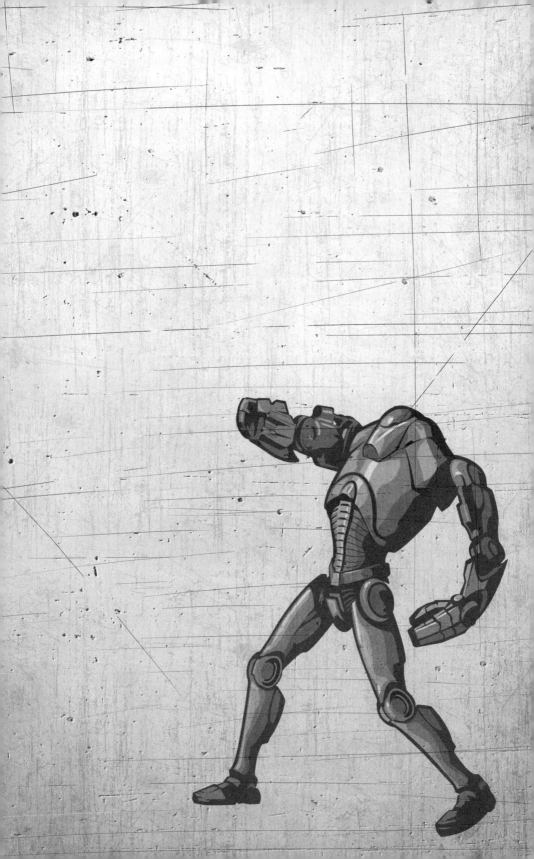

Anakin Skywalker: "What happened to him?"

Chancellor Palpatine: "He became so powerful, the only thing he was afraid of was losing his power. Which, eventually, of course, he did. Unfortunately, he taught his apprentice everything he knew and then his apprentice killed him in his sleep. Ironic…he could save others from death but not himself."

Anakin Skywalker: "Is it possible to learn this power?"
Chancellor Palpatine: "Not from a Jedi."

Chancellor Palpatine: "It is upsetting to me to see that the Council doesn't seem to fully appreciate your talents. Don't you wonder why they won't <u>make you a</u> Jedi Master?"

Anakin Skywalker: "<u>I wish I knew.</u> More and more I get the feeling that I am being excluded from the Council. I know there are things about the Force that they are not telling me."

Chancellor Palpatine: "They don't trust you, Anakin. They see your future. They know your power will be too strong to control. Anakin, you must break through the fog of lies the Jedi have created around you. Let me help you to know the subtleties of the Force."

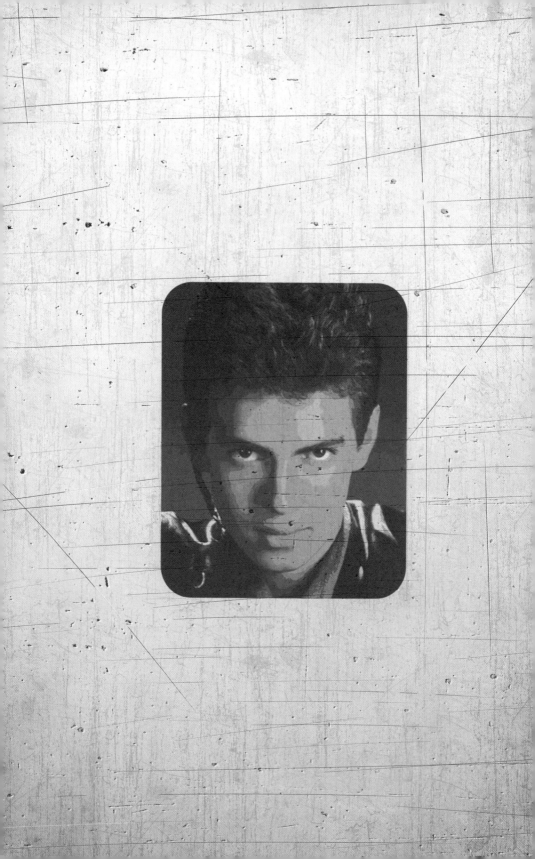

Anakin Skywalker: "How do you know the ways of the Force?"

Chancellor Palpatine: "My mentor taught me everything about the Force...even the nature of the dark side."

Anakin Skywalker: "You know the dark side?"

Chancellor Palpatine: "Anakin, if one is to understand the great mystery, one must study all its aspects, not just the dogmatic, narrow view of the Jedi. If you wish to become a complete and wise leader, you must embrace a larger view of the Force."

Chancellor Palpatine: "Only through me can you achieve a power greater than any Jedi. Learn to know the dark side of the Force, Anakin, and you will be able to save your wife from certain death."

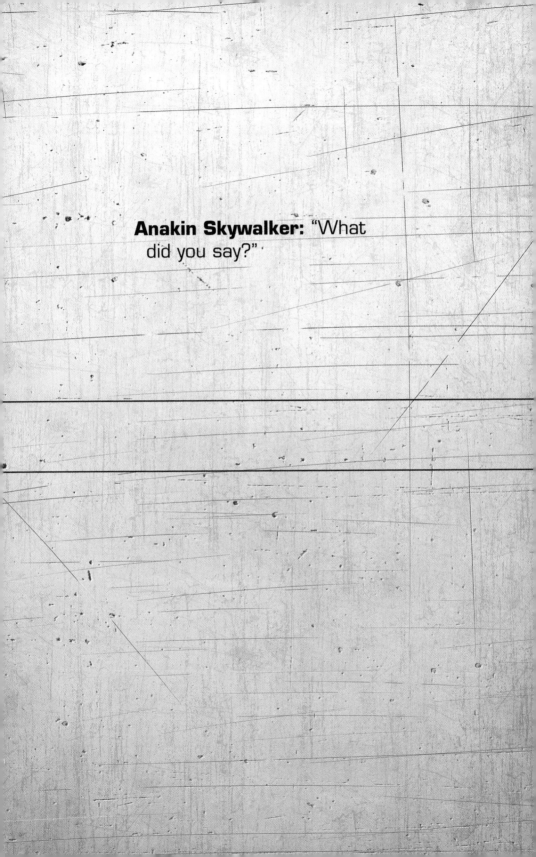

Anakin Skywalker: "What did you say?"

DARTH VADER

Chancellor Palpatine: "Use my knowledge, I beg you…"

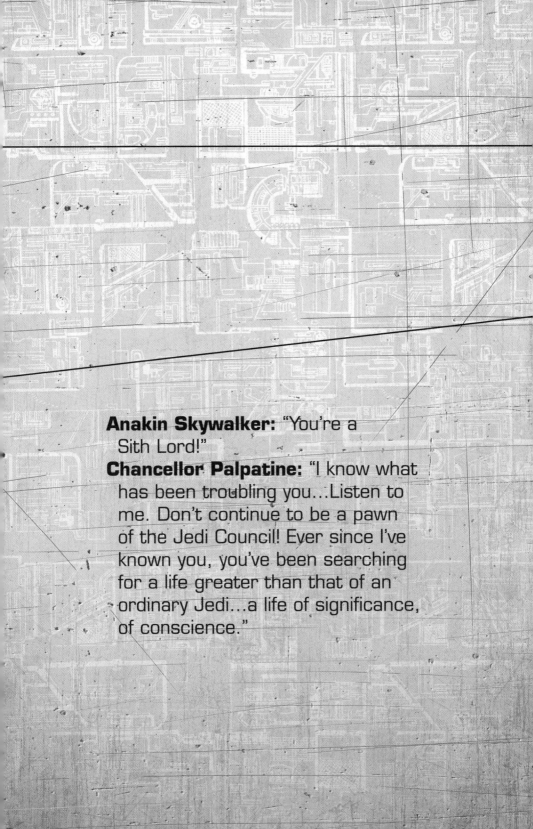

Anakin Skywalker: "You're a Sith Lord!"

Chancellor Palpatine: "I know what has been troubling you...Listen to me. Don't continue to be a pawn of the Jedi Council! Ever since I've known you, you've been searching for a life greater than that of an ordinary Jedi...a life of significance, of conscience."

Mace Windu: "In the name of the Galactic Senate of the Republic, you are under arrest, Chancellor."
Chancellor Palpatine: "Are you threatening me, Master Jedi?"

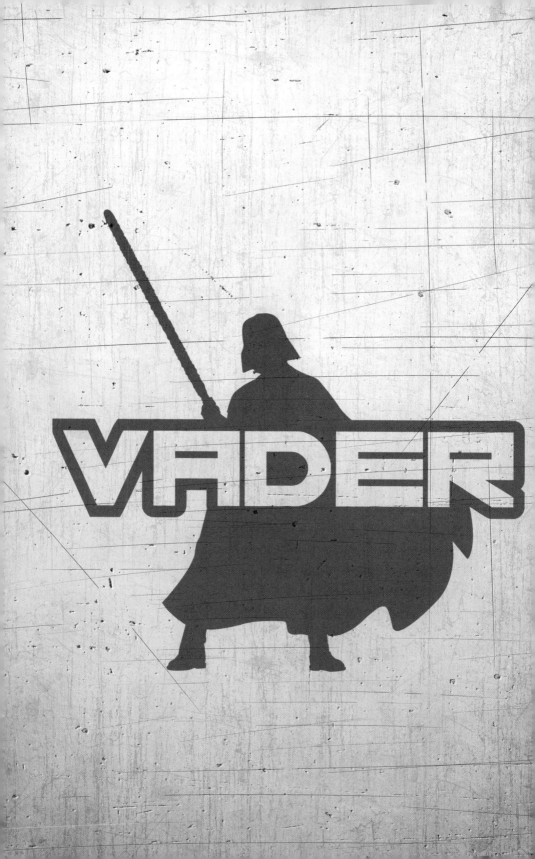

Mace Windu: "The Senate will decide your fate."

Chancellor Palpatine: "I AM the Senate."

Mace Windu: "Not yet."

Chancellor Palpatine: "It's treason, then."

Mace Windu: "You are under arrest, my Lord."

Chancellor Palpatine: "Anakin!
   I told you it would come to
   this. I was right. The Jedi are
   taking over!"

Mace Windu: "The oppression of the Sith will never return. You have lost."

Chancellor Palpatine: "No, no, no!
You will die!"

Chancellor Palpatine: "I have the power to save the ones you love. You must choose!"

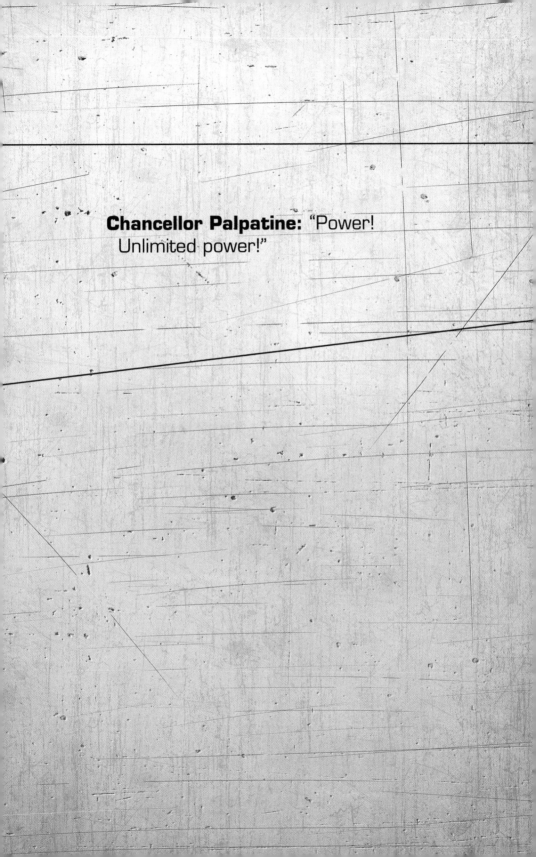

Chancellor Palpatine: "Power! Unlimited power!"

Anakin Skywalker: "What have I done?"

Chancellor Palpatine: "You're fulfilling your destiny, Anakin. Become my apprentice. Learn to use the dark side of the Force."

Anakin Skywalker: "I will do whatever you ask."
Chancellor Palpatine: "Good."

Anakin Skywalker: "Just help me save Padme's life. I can't live without her."

Chancellor Palpatine: "To cheat death is a power only one has achieved, but if we work together I know we can discover the secret."

Anakin Skywalker: "I pledge myself to your teachings."

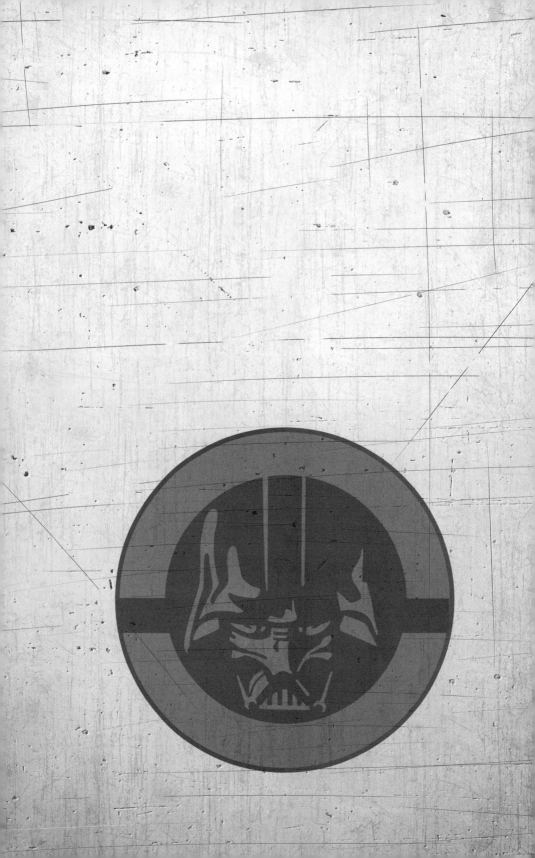

Chancellor Palpatine: "The Force is strong with you. A powerful Sith you will become."

Chancellor Palpatine: "Henceforth, you shall be known as Darth Vader."
Darth Vader: "Thank you, my Master."

Chancellor Palpatine: "Every single Jedi, including your friend Obi-Wan Kenobi, is now an enemy of the Republic."

Chancellor Palpatine: "We must move quickly. The Jedi are relentless. If they are not all destroyed, it will be civil war without end. First, I want you to go to the Jedi Temple. We will catch them off balance. Do what must be done, Lord Vader. Do not hesitate. Show no mercy."

Darth Vader: "What about the other Jedi spread across the galaxy?"

Chancellor Palpatine: "Their betrayal will be dealt with. After you have killed all the Jedi in the Temple, go to the Mustafar system. Wipe out Viceroy Gunray and the other Separatist leaders. Once more the Sith will rule the galaxy. And we shall have peace."

Emperor Palpatine: "Execute Order 66."

Yoda: "I hear a new apprentice you have, Emperor. Or should I call you Darth Sidious."

Emperor Palpatine: "Master Yoda. You survived."
Yoda: "Surprised?"

Emperor Palpatine: "Your arrogance blinds you, Master. Now you will experience the full power of the dark side."

Emperor Palpatine: "I have waited a long time for this moment, my little green friend."

Emperor Palpatine: "At last the Jedi are no more."
Yoda: "Not if anything to say about it I have."

Yoda: "At an end your rule is, and not short enough it was."

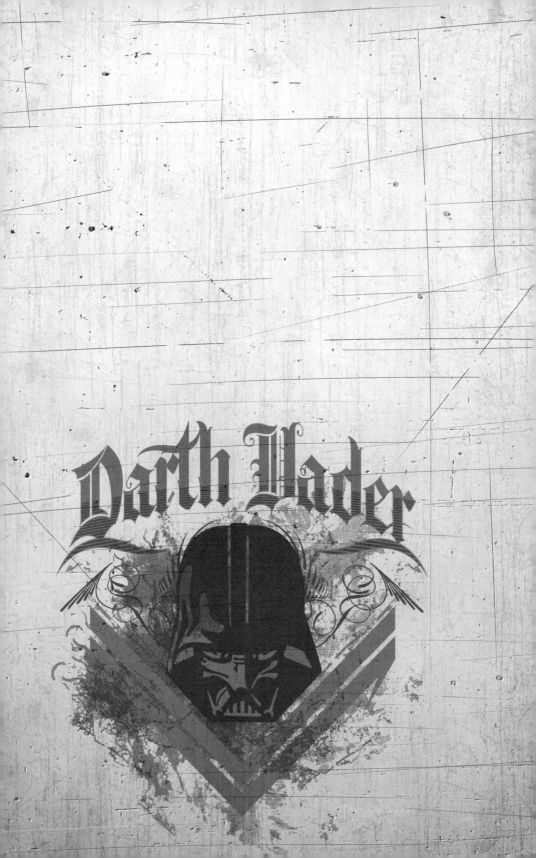

Yoda: "If so powerful you are, why leave?"

Emperor Palpatine: "You will not stop me. Darth Vader will become more powerful than either of us."

Yoda: "Faith in your new apprentice, misplaced may be. As is your faith in the dark side of the Force."

Darth Vader: "If you're not with me, then you're my enemy."

Obi-Wan Kenobi: "Only a Sith deals in absolutes. I will do what I must."

Obi-Wan Kenobi: "I have failed you, Anakin. I have failed you."
Darth Vader: "I should have known the Jedi were plotting to take over."

Obi-Wan Kenobi: "Anakin, Chancellor Palpatine is evil!"

Darth Vader: "From my point of view, the Jedi are evil."

Obi-Wan Kenobi: "Well, then you are lost!"

Darth Vader: "This is the end for you, my Master."

Obi-Wan Kenobi: "It's over,
   Anakin. I have the high ground."
Darth Vader: "You
   underestimate my power."

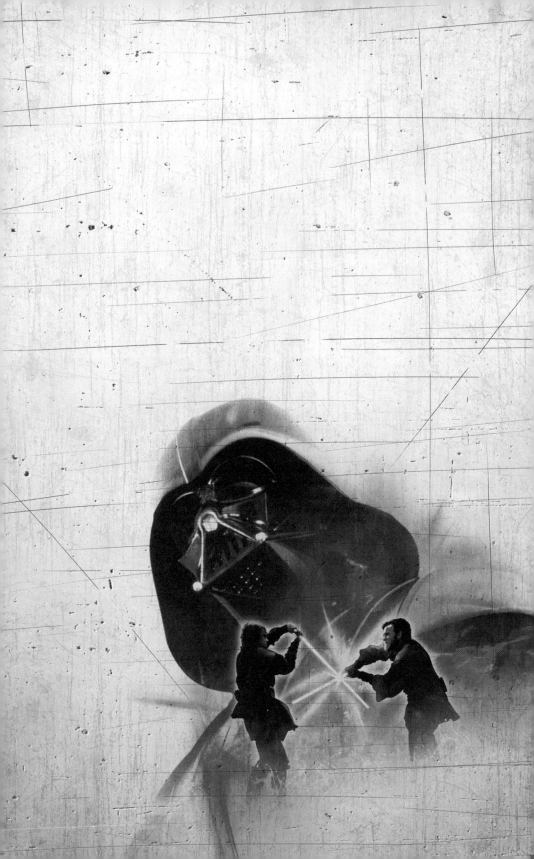

Obi-Wan Kenobi: "You were the Chosen One. It was said that you would destroy the Sith, not join them! Bring balance to the Force, not leave it in darkness!"

Darth Vader: "I hate you!"
Obi-Wan Kenobi: "You were my brother, Anakin. I loved you."

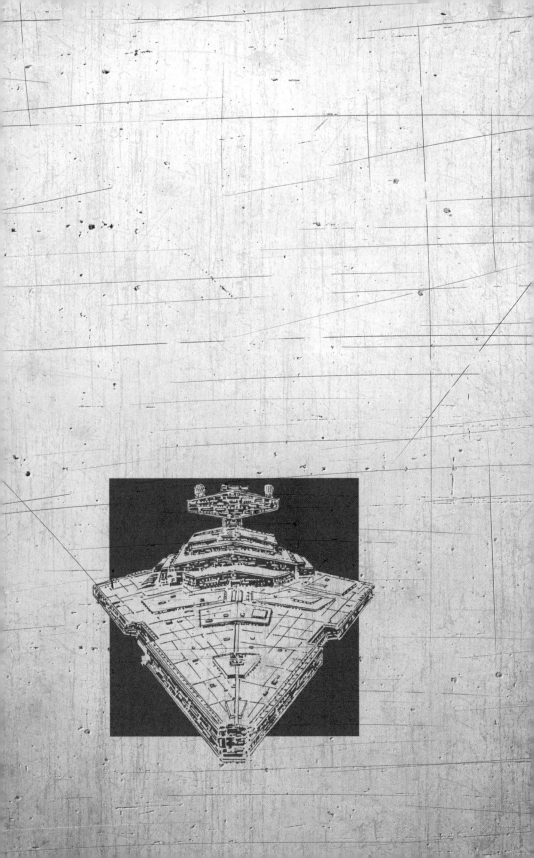

Darth Vader: "Where are those transmissions you intercepted? What have you done with those plans?"

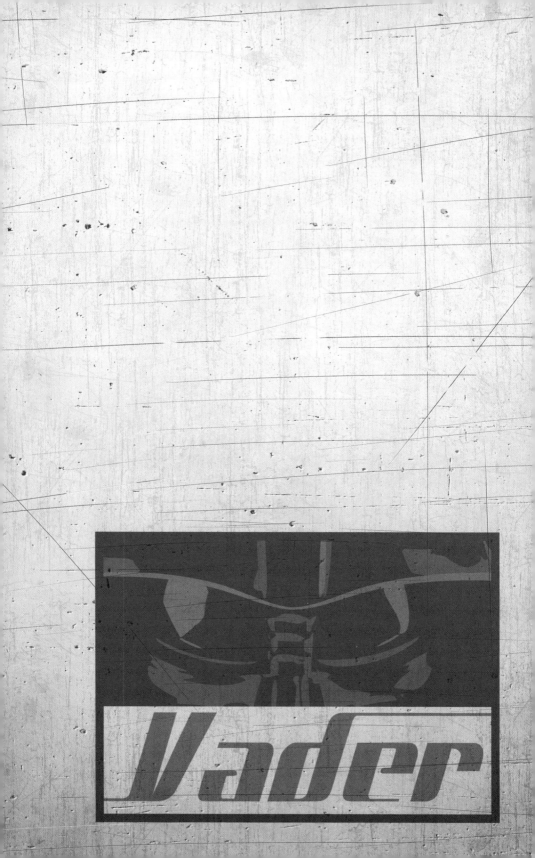

Darth Vader: "If this is a consular ship…where is the ambassador?"

Darth Vader: "Commander, tear this ship apart until you've found those plans and bring me the passengers. I want them alive!"

Princess Leia: "Darth Vader. Only you could be so bold. The Imperial Senate will not sit still for this. When they hear you've attacked a diplomatic—"

Darth Vader: "Don't act so surprised, Your Highness. You weren't on any mercy mission this time. Several transmissions were beamed to this ship by rebel spies. I want to know what happened to the plans they sent you."

Princess Leia: "I don't know what you're talking about. I'm a member of the Imperial Senate on a diplomatic mission to Alderaan."

Darth Vader: "You are part of the Rebel Alliance and a traitor. Take her away!"

Commander: "Holding her is dangerous. If word of this gets out, it could generate sympathy for the rebellion in the Senate."

Darth Vader: "I have traced the rebel spies to her. Now she is my only link to finding their secret base."

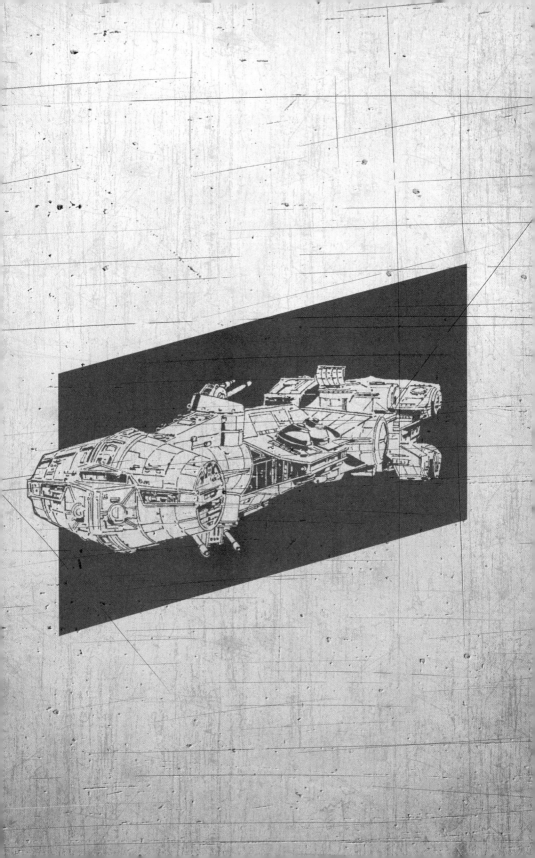

Commander: "She'll die before she'll tell you anything."

Darth Vader: "Leave that to me. Send a distress signal and then inform the Senate that all aboard were killed!"

Second Commander: "Lord Vader, the battle station plans are not aboard this ship! And no transmissions were made. An escape pod was jettisoned during the fighting, but no life-forms were aboard."

Darth Vader: "She must have hidden the plans in the escape pod. Send a detachment down to retrieve them. See to it personally, Commander. There'll be no one to stop us this time."

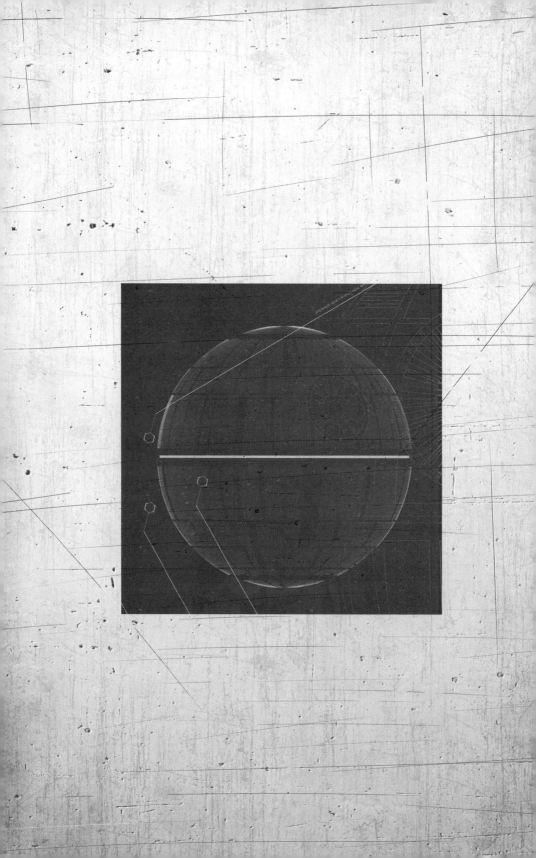

Darth Vader: "Don't be too proud of this technological terror you've constructed. The ability to destroy a planet is insignificant next to the power of the Force."

Admiral Motti: "Don't try to frighten us with your sorcerer's ways, Lord Vader. Your sad devotion to that ancient religion has not helped you conjure up the stolen data tapes or given you clairvoyance enough to find the rebels' hidden fort..."

Darth Vader: "I find your lack of faith disturbing."

Darth Vader: "And now, Your Highness, we will discuss the location of your hidden rebel base."

Luke Skywalker: "How did my father die?"

Obi-Wan Kenobi: "A young Jedi named Darth Vader, who was a pupil of mine before he turned to evil, helped the Empire hunt down and destroy the Jedi Knights. He betrayed and murdered your father. Now the Jedi are all but extinct. Vader was seduced by the dark side of the Force."

Darth Vader: "Her resistance to the mind probe is considerable. It will be some time before we can extract any information from her."

Imperial Officer: "The final checkout is completed. All systems are operational. What course shall we set?"

Grand Moff Tarkin: "Perhaps she would respond to an alternative form of persuasion."

Darth Vader: "What do you mean?"

Grand Moff Tarkin: "Set your course for Alderaan."

Princess Leia: "Governor Tarkin. I should have expected to find you holding Vader's leash. I recognized your foul stench when I was brought on board."

Darth Vader: "Did you find any droids?"

Darth Vader: "I sense something…
a presence I've not felt since…"

Darth Vader: "He is here..."

Grand Moff Tarkin: "Obi-Wan Kenobi? What makes you think so?"

Darth Vader: "A tremor in the Force. The last time I felt it was in the presence of my old Master."

Grand Moff Tarkin: "Surely he must be dead by now."

Darth Vader: "Don't underestimate the Force."

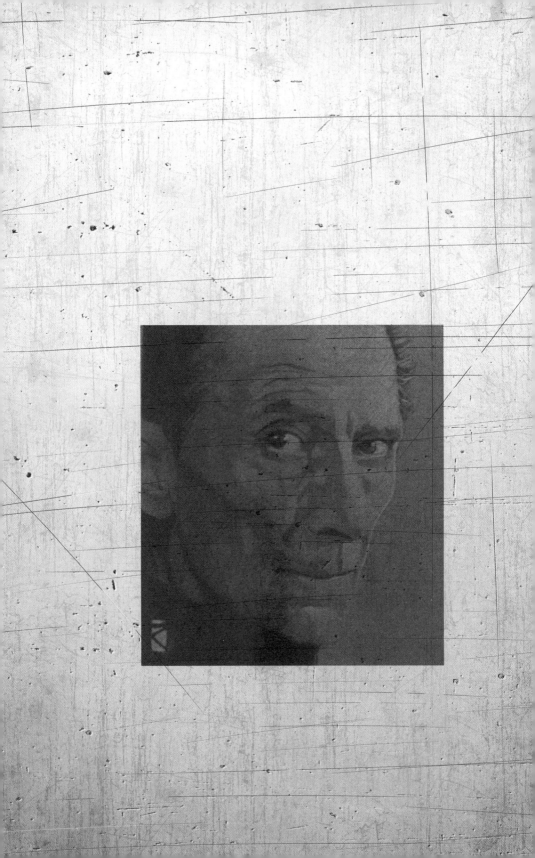

Darth Vader: "Obi-Wan is here. The Force is with him."

Grand Moff Tarkin: "If you're right, he must not be allowed to escape."

Darth Vader: "Escape is not his plan. I must face him alone."

Darth Vader: "I've been waiting for you, Obi-Wan. We meet again at last. The circle is now complete."

Darth Vader: "When I left you I was but the learner. Now I am the master."
Obi-Wan Kenobi: "Only a master of evil, Darth."

Darth Vader: "Your powers are weak, old man."

Obi-Wan Kenobi: "You can't win, Darth. If you strike me down, I shall become more powerful than you can possibly imagine."

Darth Vader: "Stay in attack formation!"

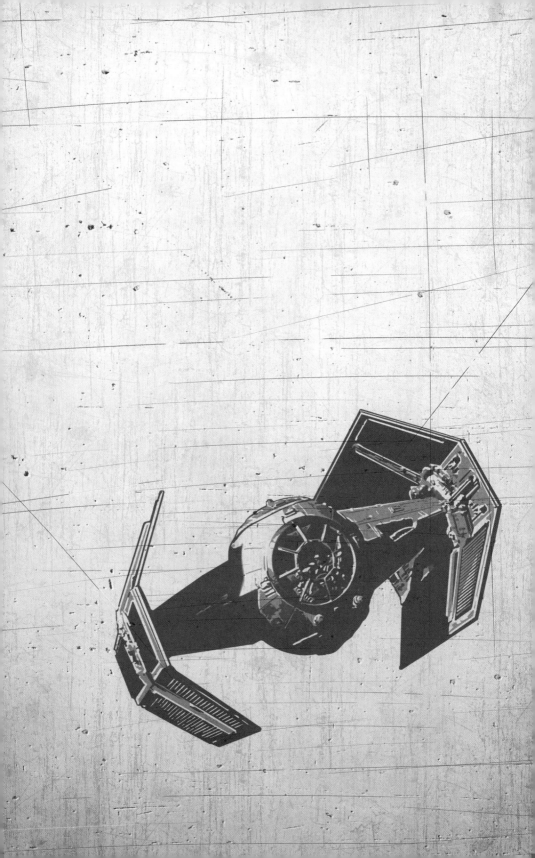

Darth Vader: "I'll take them myself. Cover me!"

Darth Vader: "The Force is strong with this one!"

Darth Vader: "You found something?"
Captain Piett: "Yes, my lord."
Darth Vader: "That's it. The rebels are there."

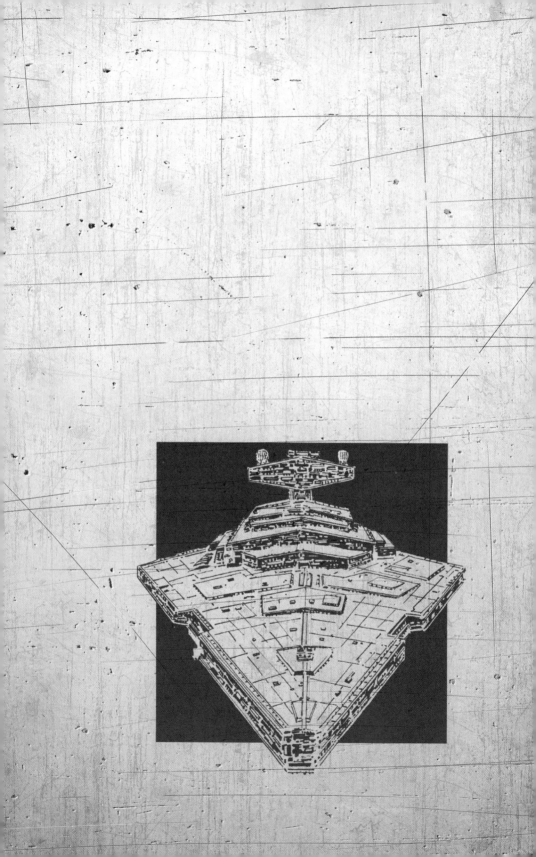

Admiral Ozzel: "My Lord, there are so many uncharted settlements. It could be smugglers, it could be…"

Darth Vader: "That is the system. And I'm sure Skywalker is with them. Set your course for the Hoth system. General Veers, prepare your men."

Darth Vader: "What is it, General?"
General Veers: "My Lord, the fleet has moved out of lightspeed. Com-scan has detected an energy field protecting an area of the sixth planet of the Hoth system. The field is strong enough to deflect any bombardment."

Darth Vader: "The rebels are alerted to our presence. Admiral Ozzel came out of lightspeed too close to the system."

General Veers: "He felt surprise was wiser…"

Darth Vader: "He is as clumsy as he is stupid. General, prepare your troops for a surface attack."

Admiral Ozzel: "Lord Vader, the fleet has moved out of lightspeed and we're preparing to…"

Darth Vader: "You have failed me for the last time, Admiral. Captain Piett."

Captain Piett: "Yes, my lord."

Darth Vader: "Make ready to land our troops beyond their energy field and deploy the fleet so that nothing gets off the system. You are in command now, Admiral Piett."

Admiral Piett: "Thank you, Lord Vader."

Darth Vader: "Yes, Admiral?"

Admiral Piett: "Our ships have sighted the *Millennium Falcon*, Lord. But…it has entered an asteroid field and we cannot risk—"

Darth Vader: "Asteroids do not concern me, Admiral. I want that ship, not excuses."

Admiral Piett: "Yes, Lord."

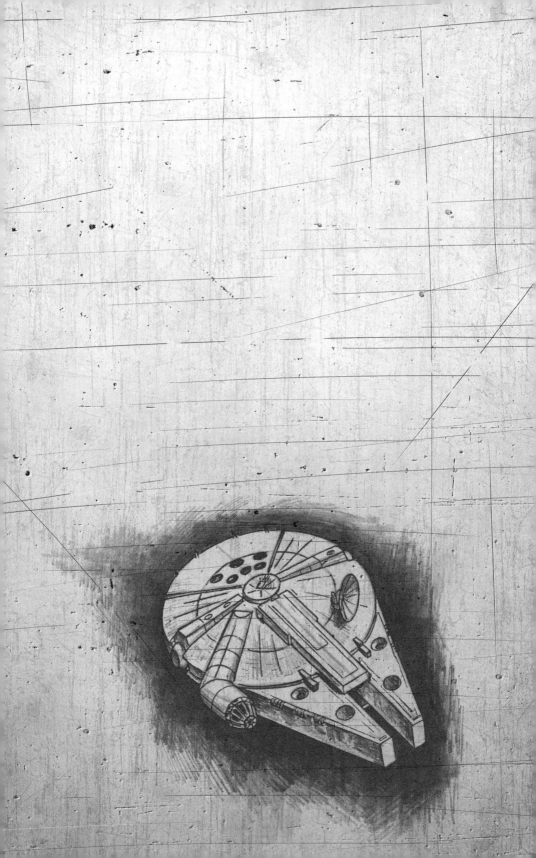

Captain Needa: "...and that, Lord Vader, was the last time they appeared in any of our scopes. Considering the amount of damage we've sustained, they must have been destroyed."

Darth Vader: "No, Captain, they're alive. I want every ship available to sweep the asteroid field until they are found."

Admiral Piett: "The Emperor commands you to make contact with him."

Darth Vader: 'Move the ship out of the asteroid field so that we can send a clear transmission."

Darth Vader: "What is thy bidding, my Master?"

Emperor Palpatine: "There is a great disturbance in the Force."

Darth Vader: "I have felt it."

Emperor Palpatine: "We have a new enemy. The young rebel who destroyed the Death Star. I have no doubt this boy is the offspring of Anakin Skywalker."

Darth Vader: "How is that possible?"

Emperor Palpatine: "Search your feelings, Lord Vader. You will know it to be true."

Emperor Palpatine: "He could destroy us."
Darth Vader: "He is just a boy. Obi-Wan can no longer help him."

Emperor Palpatine: "The Force is strong with him. The son of Skywalker must not become a Jedi."

Darth Vader: "If he could be turned, he would become a powerful ally."

Emperor Palpatine: "Yes. He would be a great asset. Can it be done?"

Darth Vader: "He will join us or die, Master."

Darth Vader: "There will be a substantial reward for the one who finds the *Millennium Falcon*. You are free to use any means necessary, but I want them alive. No disintegrations."

Boba Fett: "As you wish."

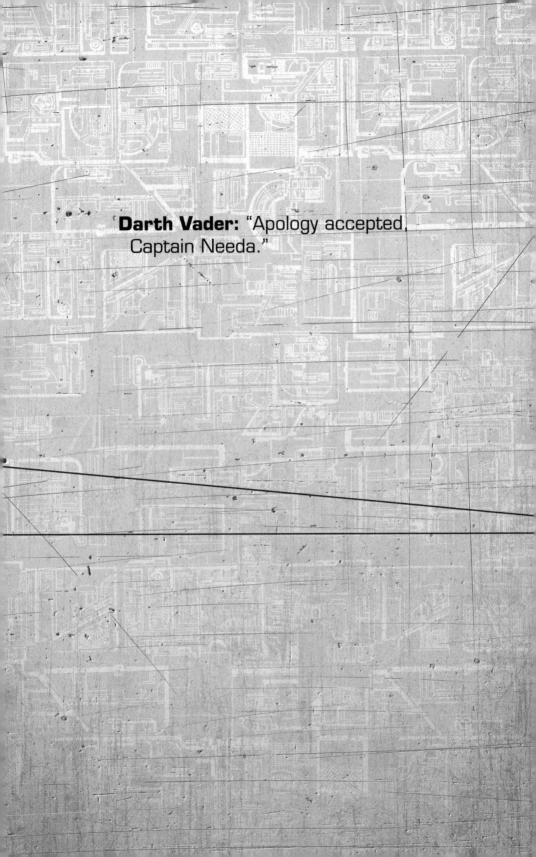

Darth Vader: "Apology accepted, Captain Needa."

Admiral Piett: "Lord Vader, our ships have completed their scan of the area and found nothing. If the *Millennium Falcon* went into lightspeed, it'll be on the other side of the galaxy by now."

Darth Vader: "Alert all commands. Calculate every possible destination along their last known trajectory."

Darth Vader: "Don't fail me again, Admiral."

Obi-Wan Kenobi: "Luke, I don't want to lose you to the Emperor the way I lost Vader."

Luke Skywalker: "You won't."

Yoda: "Stopped they must be. On
this all depends. Only a fully trained
Jedi with the Force as his ally will
conquer Vader and his Emperor.
If you end your training now, if you
choose the quick and easy path,
as Vader did, you will become an
agent of evil."

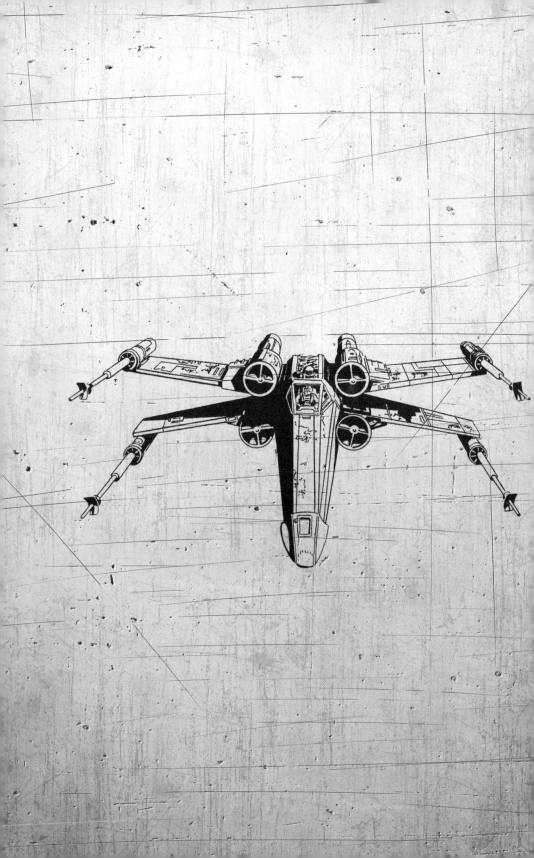

Obi-Wan Kenobi: "If you choose to fight Vader, you will do it alone. I cannot interfere."

Yoda: "Strong is Vader. Mind what you have learned. Save you it can."

Darth Vader: "We would be honored if you would join us."

Darth Vader: "You may take Captain Solo to Jabba the Hutt after I have Skywalker."

Boba Fett: "He's no good to me dead."

Darth Vader: "He will not be permanently damaged."

Lando Calrissian: "Lord Vader, what about Leia and the Wookiee?"

Darth Vader: "They must never again leave this city."

Lando Calrissian: "That was never a condition of our agreement, nor was giving Han to this bounty hunter!"

Darth Vader: "Perhaps you feel you're being treated unfairly?"

Lando Calrissian: "No."

Darth Vader: "Good. It would be unfortunate if I had to leave a garrison here."

Darth Vader: "This facility is crude, but it should be adequate to freeze Skywalker for his journey to the Emperor."

Lando Calrissian: "Lord Vader, we only use this facility for carbon freezing. You put him in there...it might kill him."

Darth Vader: "I do not want the Emperor's prize damaged. We will test it...on Captain Solo."

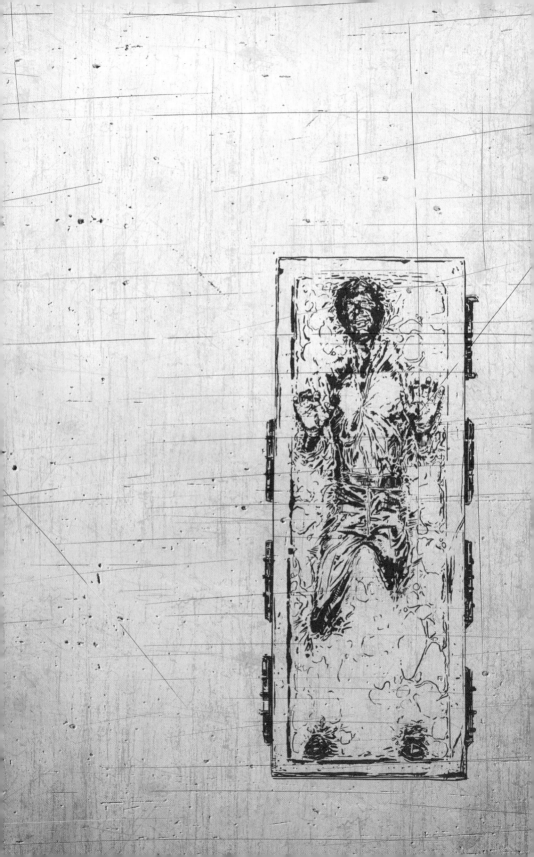

Boba Fett: "What if he doesn't survive? He's worth a lot to me."

Darth Vader: "The Empire will compensate you if he dies. Put him in!"

Imperial Officer: "Skywalker has just landed, my Lord."
Darth Vader: "Good. See to it that he finds his way in here."

Darth Vader: "Calrissian, take the princess and the Wookiee to my ship."

Lando Calrissian: "You said they'd be left in the city under my supervision."

Darth Vader: "I am altering the deal. Pray I don't alter it any further."

Darth Vader: "The Force is with you, young Skywalker. But you are not a Jedi yet."

Darth Vader: "You have learned much, young one."

Luke Skywalker: "You'll find I'm full of surprises."

Darth Vader: "Your destiny lies with me, Skywalker. Obi-Wan knew this to be true."

Darth Vader: "All too easy.
Perhaps you are not as strong
as the Emperor thought."

Darth Vader: "Impressive.
Most impressive."

Darth Vader: "Obi-Wan has taught you well. You have controlled your fear…now release your anger. Only your hatred can destroy me."

Darth Vader: "You are beaten. It is useless to resist. Don't let yourself be destroyed as Obi-Wan did."

Darth Vader: "There is no escape. Don't make me destroy you, Luke. You do not yet realize your importance. You have only begun to discover your power. Join me and I will complete your training. With our combined strength, we can end this destructive conflict and bring order to the galaxy."

Luke Skywalker: "I'll never join you."
Darth Vader: "If you only knew the power of the dark side. Obi-Wan never told you what happened to your father."

Luke Skywalker: "He told me enough. He told me you killed him."
Darth Vader: "No. I am your father."

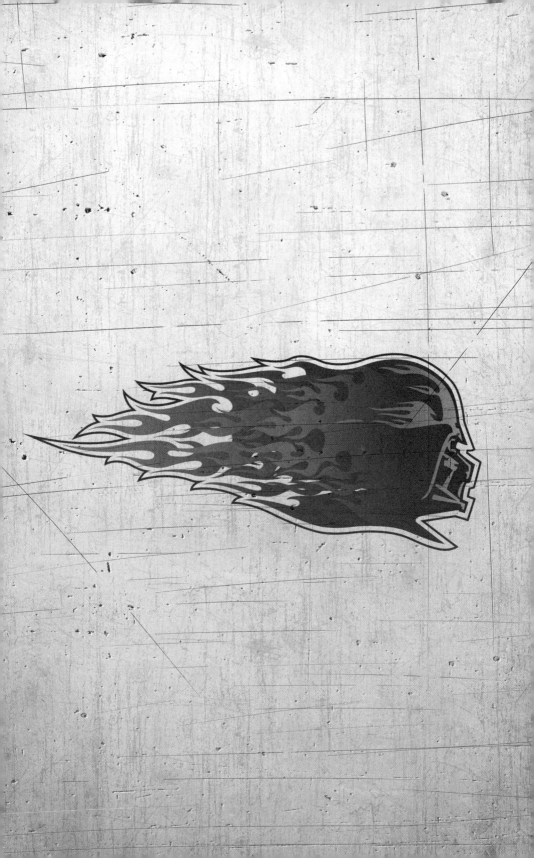

Luke Skywalker: "That's not true. That's impossible!"
Darth Vader: "Search your feelings. You know it to be true."

Darth Vader: "Luke. You can destroy the Emperor. He has foreseen this. It is your destiny. Join me, and together we can rule the galaxy as father and son."

Darth Vader: "Come with
me. It is the only way."

Darth Vader: "Luke…it is your destiny."

Commander Jerjerrod:
"Lord Vader, this is an
unexpected pleasure.
We're honored by
your presence."

Darth Vader: "You may
dispense with the
pleasantries, Commander.
I'm here to put you back
on schedule."

VADER

Commander Jerjerrod: "I assure you, Lord Vader, my men are working as fast as they can."
Darth Vader: "Perhaps I can find new ways to motivate them."

Commander Jerjerrod: "I tell you, this station will be operational as planned."

Darth Vader: "The Emperor does not share your optimistic appraisal of the situation."

Commander Jerjerrod: "But he asks the impossible. I need more men."

Darth Vader: "Then perhaps you can tell him when he arrives."

Commander Jerjerrod: "The Emperor's coming here?"
Darth Vader: "That is correct, commander. And he is most displeased with your apparent lack of progress."

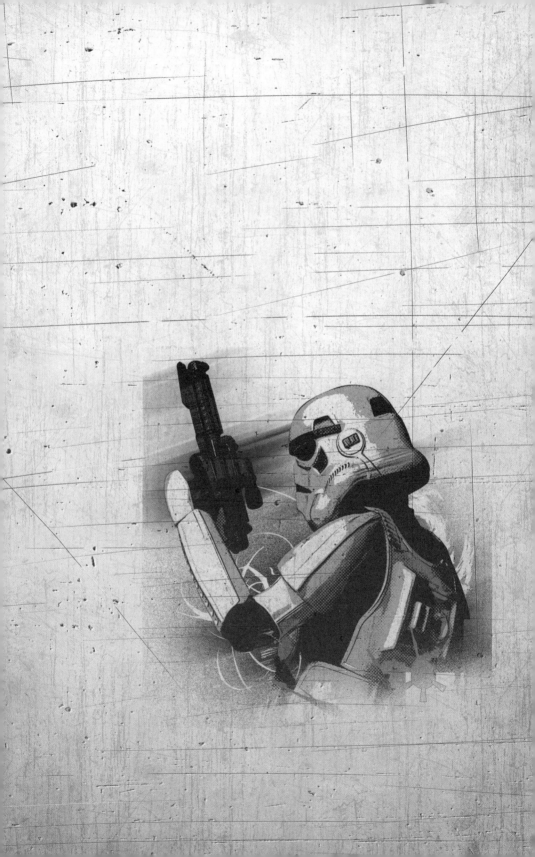

Commander Jerjerrod: "We shall double our efforts."
Darth Vader: "I hope so, Commander, for your sake. The Emperor is not as forgiving as I am."

Darth Vader: "The Death Star will be completed on schedule."

Emperor Palpatine: "You have done well, Lord Vader. And now, I sense you wish to continue your search for young Skywalker."

Darth Vader: "Yes, my Master."

Emperor Palpatine: "Patience, my friend. In time he will seek you out. And when he does, you must bring him before me. He has grown strong. Only together can we turn him to the dark side of the Force."

Darth Vader: "As you wish."

Emperor Palpatine: "Everything is proceeding as I have foreseen."

Luke Skywalker: "Master Yoda... is Darth Vader my father?"

Yoda: "Mmm...rest I need. Yes... rest."

Luke Skywalker: "Yoda, I must know."

Yoda: "Your father he is. Told you, did he?"

Luke Skywalker: "Yes."

Luke Skywalker: "Obi-Wan! Why didn't you tell me? You told me Vader betrayed and murdered my father."

Obi-Wan Kenobi: "Your father was seduced by the dark side of the Force. He ceased to be Anakin Skywalker and became Darth Vader. When that happened, the good man that was your father was destroyed. So what I told you was true...from a certain point of view."

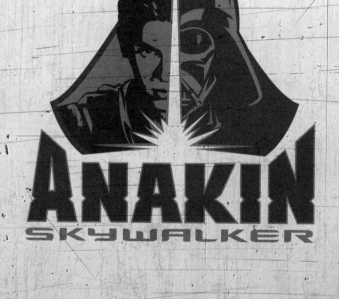

ANAKIN
SKYWALKER

Obi-Wan Kenobi: "Anakin was a good friend. When I first knew him, your father was already a great pilot. But I was amazed how strongly the Force was with him. I took it upon myself to train him as a Jedi. I thought that I could instruct him just as well as Yoda. I was wrong."

Luke Skywalker: "There is still good in him."

Obi-Wan Kenobi: "He's more machine now than man. Twisted and evil."

Darth Vader: "What is thy bidding, my Master?"

Emperor Palpatine: "Send the fleet to the far side of Endor. There it will stay until called for."

Darth Vader: "What of the reports of the rebel fleet massing near Sullust?"

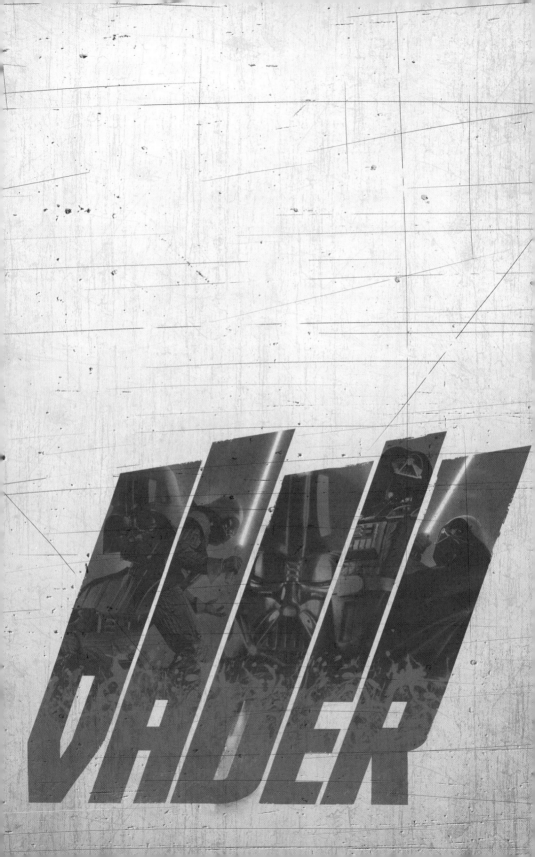

Emperor Palpatine: "It is of no concern. Soon the rebellion will be crushed and young Skywalker will be one of us. Your work here is finished, my friend. Go out to the command ship and await my orders."

Darth Vader: "Yes, my Master."

Emperor Palpatine: "I told you to remain on the command ship."
Darth Vader: "A small rebel force has penetrated the shield and landed on Endor."

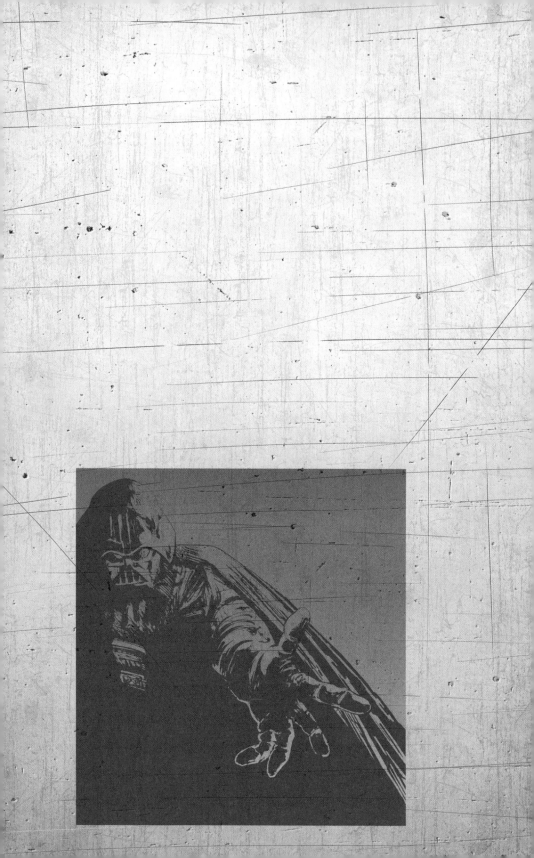

Emperor Palpatine: "Yes, I know."
Darth Vader: "My son is with them."
Emperor Palpatine: "Are you sure?"
Darth Vader: "I have felt him, my Master."

Emperor Palpatine: "Strange that I have not. I wonder if your feelings on this matter are clear, Lord Vader."

Darth Vader: "They are clear, my Master."

Emperor Palpatine: "Then you must go to the Sanctuary Moon and wait for him."

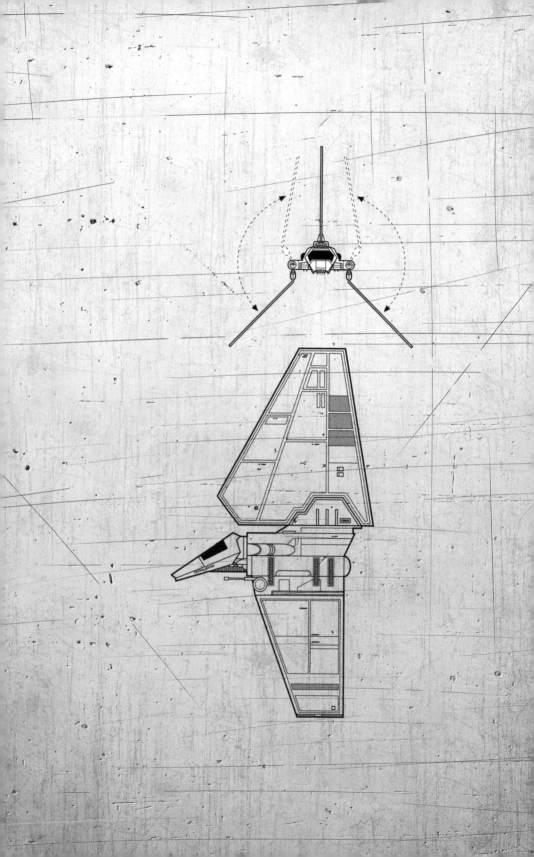

Darth Vader: "He will come to me?"
Emperor Palpatine: "I have foreseen it. His compassion for you will be his undoing. He will come to you, and then you will bring him before me."
Darth Vader: "As you wish."

Luke Skywalker: "Vader is here...
now, on this moon."
Princess Leia: "How do you know?"
Luke Skywalker: "I felt his presence.
He's come for me. He can feel when
I'm near. That's why I have to go. As
long as I stay, I'm endangering the
group and our mission here."
Princess Leia: "Why?"
Luke Skywalker: "He's my father."

Princess Leia: "But why must you confront him?"

Luke Skywalker: "Because…there is good in him. I've felt it. He won't turn me over to the Emperor. I can save him. I can turn him back to the good side. I have to try."

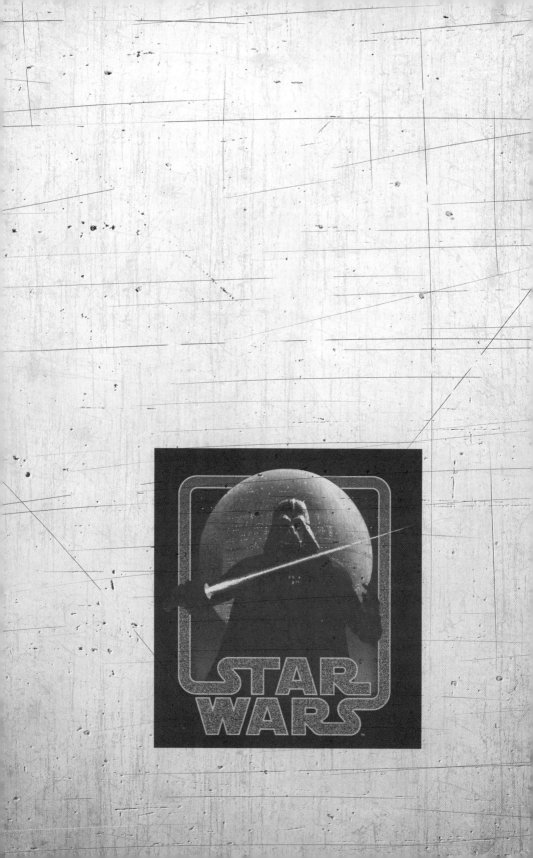

Darth Vader: "The Emperor has been expecting you."
Luke Skywalker: "I know, father."

Darth Vader: "So you have accepted the truth."

Luke Skywalker: "I've accepted that you were once Anakin Skywalker, my father."

Darth Vader: "That name no longer has any meaning for me."

Luke Skywalker: "It is the name of your true self. You've only forgotten. I know there is good in you. The Emperor hasn't driven it from you fully. That was why you couldn't destroy me. That's why you won't bring me to your Emperor now."

Darth Vader: "I see you have constructed a new lightsaber. Your skills are complete. Indeed, you are powerful, as the Emperor has foreseen."

Luke Skywalker: "Come with me."

Darth Vader: "Obi-Wan once thought as you do. You don't know the power of the dark side. I must obey my Master."

Luke Skywalker: "I will not turn...and you'll be forced to kill me."
Darth Vader: "If that is your destiny..."

Luke Skywalker: "Search your feelings, father. You can't do this. I feel the conflict within you. Let go of your hate."

Darth Vader: "It is too late for me, son. The Emperor will show you the true nature of the Force. He is your Master now."

Luke Skywalker: "Then my father is truly dead."

Emperor Palpatine: "I'm looking forward to completing your training. In time you will call me Master."

Luke Skywalker: "You're gravely mistaken. You won't convert me as you did my father."

Emperor Palpatine: "Oh, no, my young Jedi. You will find that it is you who are mistaken...about a great many things."

Darth Vader: "His lightsaber."

Emperor Palpatine: "Ah, yes, a Jedi's weapon. Much like your father's. By now you must know your father can never be turned from the dark side. So will it be with you."

Luke Skywalker: "You're wrong. Soon I'll be dead...and you with me."

Emperor Palpatine: "Perhaps you refer to the imminent attack of your rebel fleet."

Emperor Palpatine: "Yes…I assure you. We are quite safe from your friends here."

Luke Skywalker: "Your overconfidence is your weakness."

Emperor Palpatine: "Your faith in your friends is yours."

Darth Vader: "It is pointless to resist, my son."

Emperor Palpatine: "Everything that has transpired has done so according to my design. Your friends up there on the Sanctuary Moon are walking into a trap. As is your rebel fleet! It was I who allowed the Alliance to know the location of the shield generator. It is quite safe from your pitiful little band. An entire legion of my best troops awaits them."

Emperor Palpatine: "Oh, I'm afraid the deflector shield will be quite operational when your friends arrive."

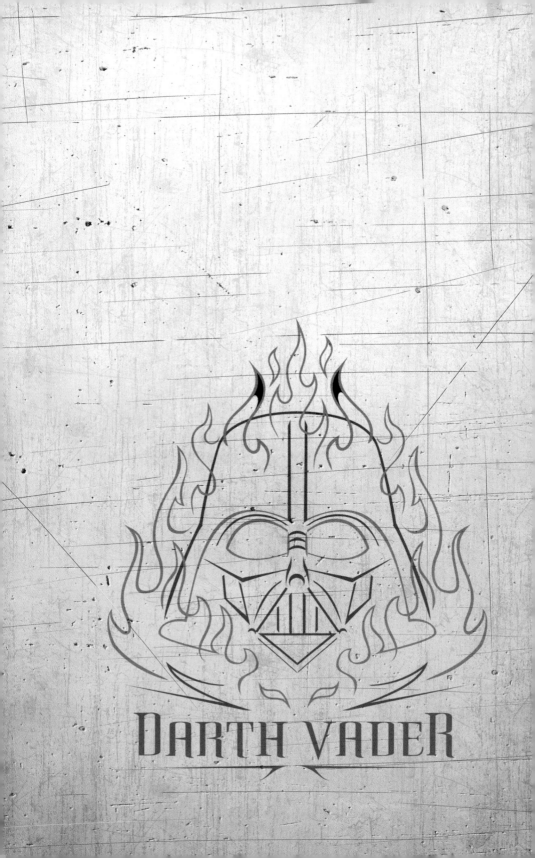

DARTH VADER

Emperor Palpatine: "You want this, don't you? The hate is swelling in you now. Take your Jedi weapon. Use it. I am unarmed. Strike me down with it. Give in to your anger. With each passing moment you make yourself more my servant."

Luke Skywalker: "No!"

Emperor Palpatine: "It is unavoidable. It is your destiny. You, like your father, are now mine."

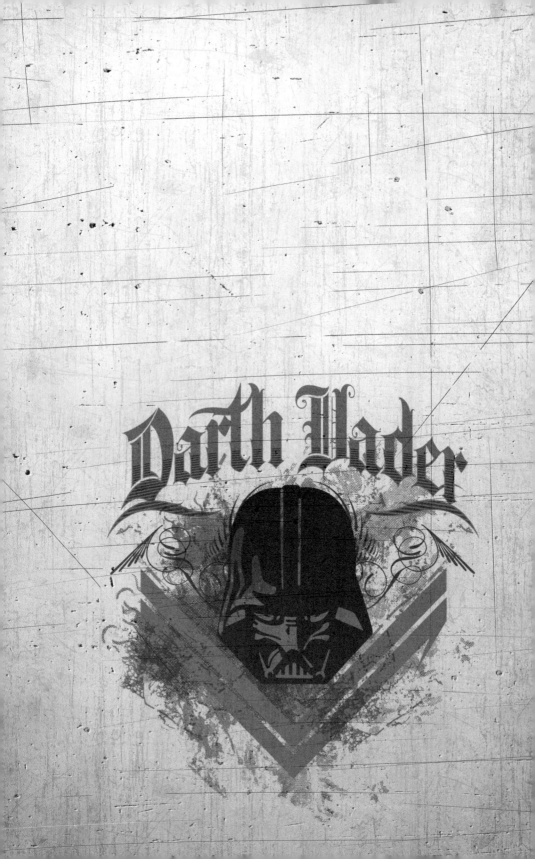

Emperor Palpatine: "Your fleet is lost. And your friends on the Endor moon will not survive. There is no escape, my young apprentice. The Alliance will die... as will your friends."

Emperor Palpatine: "Good. I can feel your anger. I am defenseless. Take your weapon! Strike me down with all of your hatred and your journey toward the dark side will be complete."

Darth Vader: "Obi-Wan has taught you well."

Luke Skywalker: "I will not fight you, father."

Darth Vader: "You are unwise to lower your defenses."

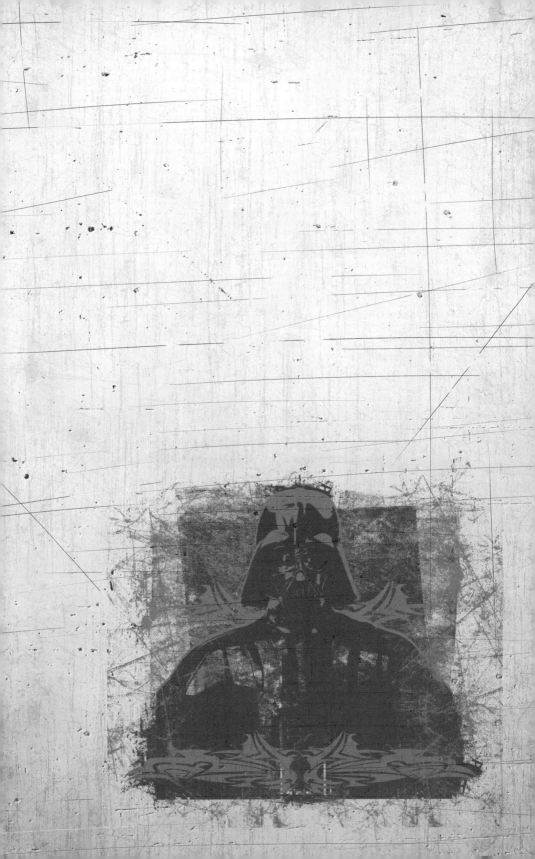

Luke Skywalker: "Your thoughts betray you, father. I feel the good in you…the conflict."
Darth Vader: "There is no conflict."

Luke Skywalker: "You couldn't bring yourself to kill me before, and I don't believe you'll destroy me now."

Darth Vader: "You underestimate the power of the dark side. If you will not fight, then you will meet your destiny."

Darth Vader: "You cannot hide forever, Luke."
Luke Skywalker: "I will not fight you."

Darth Vader: "Give yourself to the dark side. It is the only way you can save your friends."

Darth Vader: "Yes, your thoughts betray you. Your feelings for them are strong. Especially for...sister!

Darth Vader: "So…you have a twin sister. Your feelings have now betrayed her, too. Obi-Wan was wise to hide her from me. Now his failure is complete. If you will not turn to the dark side, then perhaps she will."

Emperor Palpatine: "Good! Your hate has made you powerful. Now, fulfill your destiny and take your father's place at my side."

Luke Skywalker: "Never! I'll never turn to the dark side. You've failed, Your Highness."

Luke Skywalker: "I am a Jedi, like my father before me."
Emperor Palpatine: "So be it…Jedi."

Emperor Palpatine: "If you will not be turned, you will be destroyed."

Emperor Palpatine: "Young fool…only now, at the end, do you understand."

Emperor Palpatine: "Your feeble skills are no match for the power of the dark side. You have paid the price of your lack of vision."

Darth Vader: "Luke, help me take this mask off."
Luke Skywalker: "But you'll die."

Darth Vader: "Nothing can stop that now. Just for once let me look on you with my own eyes."

Anakin Skywalker: "Now...go, my son. Leave me."

Luke Skywalker: "No. You're coming with me. I'll not leave you here. I've got to save you."

Anakin Skywalker: "You already have, Luke. You were right. You were right about me. Tell your sister...you were right."

About the Designer

The sculpture design in this edition was created exclusively for ArtFolds by Luciana Frigerio. Based in Vermont, Luciana has been making photographs, objects, book sculptures, and artistic mischief for over 30 years. Her work has been exhibited in galleries and museums around the world. Luciana's artwork can be found at: lucianafrigerio.com, and her unique, customized book sculptures can be found in her shop on the online crafts market Etsy at: etsy.com/shop/LucianaFrigerio.

The ArtFolds Portfolio

Color Editions

These smaller ArtFolds® editions use a range of colors printed on each page to make each sculpture a multi-colored work of art. Titles now or soon available include:

Edition 1: Heart
Edition 2: Mickey Mouse
Edition 3: Christmas Tree
Edition 4: MOM
Edition 5: Flower
Edition 6: Yoda

Classic Editions

These larger ArtFolds® editions include the full text of a classic book; when folded, book text appears along the edges, creating a piece of art that celebrates the dignity and beauty of a printed book. Titles now or soon available include:

Edition 1: LOVE
Edition 2: Snowflake
Edition 3: JOY
Edition 4: READ
Edition 5: Sun
Edition 6: Darth Vader

To see the full range of ArtFolds editions,
visit artfolds.com.